Hoops and Me

by Dr. L. David Furr
Illustrated by Tom Simonton

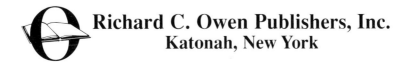

Richard C. Owen Publishers, Inc.
Katonah, New York

There isn't much to do in our neighborhood.
Sometimes we play games. Sometimes we shoot baskets
over at the school. Most of the time after school,
we just hang out and talk.

We talk about video games and sports.
We like talking about basketball the most
because one of the best basketball players
in the whole world grew up in our neighborhood.
He doesn't live here anymore, but he used to.

My mom said he still comes back here sometimes,
but I've never seen him. It would be great
to see him.

He's about ten feet tall and can jump twenty feet
off the ground. At least, that's what they say.

Now that school is out for the summer,
there aren't as many kids around to play with.
Some go to camp, some stay at their
grandmother's house.
I don't know where the rest of them are.
Most of the time, there's just me.

Almost every day I go over to the schoolyard
and shoot a few baskets. I take a long walk
around the neighborhood to see if I can find
some of my friends. I go home, get a snack,
and maybe watch some TV. Then, I'm back
on the street looking for something to do.

One day as I was crossing the street
to the schoolyard, I stopped dead in my tracks.
I couldn't believe what I was seeing.
It was money, a hundred-dollar bill!
I picked it up.

I could feel my heart pounding in my chest.
This was the most money I had ever seen
in my whole life. I was happy and scared
at the same time.

I ran home and showed my mom.
She said, "If no one asks for it by this weekend,
we'll go out and buy something really nice."

The next day was just another boring day.
The only difference was that now I was rich!
I thought and thought about what I would buy
with the money.

I went by the school. As usual, no one was there.
I shot a few baskets. I made all of them,
and started to leave. Just as I went out the gate,
a car pulled up to the curb.

The door opened and a man and a little boy
got out of the car. The man looked about ten feet tall.
He asked if he could take a couple of shots
with my basketball while his son watched.

I handed him the ball.

He took it and said, "Come on, kid."

He ran over to the basket and JAMMED the ball!

BAM! WHAM! I couldn't believe it!

He jumped straight up and jammed it again.

His feet were right next to my face when he jumped.

That man could jump twenty feet in the air!

At least, it seemed like that.

I told him that a very famous basketball player
named Hoops Johnson used to play ball in this schoolyard.
You will never believe what he told me.

He said, "I know. That's me, Derrick Johnson."

I was more nervous than when I found the money.

Hoops shot a few more baskets. Then we sat down on the sidewalk with his little son and we talked.

He wanted to know how I did in school and if I listened to my mom. Then he said, "School is important. You can't be a star basketball player unless you are a good reader. Basketball plays are written and you have to be able to read them really well."

I didn't know that.

Then Hoops had to go. He waved and said, "Be good."

When I told my mom, she couldn't believe it.
She had me tell her what happened over and over.
She was as excited as I was.

After dinner we sat together and talked about
how maybe one day I could be like Hoops.
Then we talked about what we might buy
with the money I had found. I was thinking about toys.
Mom was thinking about clothes.

The weekend finally arrived. No one anywhere
had asked about the money, so we went to the big store
that sells everything. I was excited! Mom talked clothes,
I talked toys. Mom said I could buy just one toy
and put the rest of the money in the bank.
She said it's important to learn to save money.

I decided on a new basketball. My old one
was really beat. We paid for it and went home.

As we were walking back home, we heard
a car horn blow. Guess what!
It was Hoops Johnson's car.

He stopped the car, got out, and said,
"I wanted to show my family the old neighborhood
and my old school."

He introduced us to his wife.

"Hey," he said, "is that a new ball? Can I see it?"
He spun it on his finger.

Then he took a pen out of his jacket pocket
and signed my ball. He wrote,
To my basketball playing partner.
Your friend, Derrick "Hoops" Johnson.

As Hoops was getting into his car, he said,
"Listen kid, you only have to know two things
to be successful in life.
First, go to school every day and do the best you can.
Second, always listen to your mom."

Then he winked and drove away.

I haven't seen Hoops since, except on TV.
But I remember what he told me.

I go to school every day and I do the best I can.
And I always try to listen to my mom.

Now, whenever I'm sad or lonely,
I think about Hoops and me.